For my good friend Joan—C. F.

For Jeff, for your love and encouragement—A. E.

Copyright © 2008 by Good Books, Intercourse, PA 17534
International Standard Book Number: 978-1-56148-588-8

Library of Congress Catalog Card Number: 2007004324

Text copyright © Claire Freedman 2007
Illustrations copyright © Alison Edgson 2007
Original edition published in English by Little Tiger Press,
an imprint of Magi Publications, London, England, 2007.
Printed in Singapore

Library of Congress Cataloging-in-Publication Data

Freedman, Claire.
Follow that bear if you dare! / Claire Freedman ; illustrated by Alison Edgson.
p. cm.

Summary: Hare and Rabbit bravely venture off on a bear hunt together,
carefully following the instructions in Hare's "Best Book of Bear Hunting."
ISBN: 978-1-56148-588-8 (hardcover)
[1. Hares--Fiction. 2. Rabbits--Fiction. 3. Bears--Fiction.]
I. Edgson, Alison, ill. II. Title.

PZ7.F87275Fo 2008
[E]--dc22
2007004324

FOLLOW THAT BEAR

IF YOU DARE!

Claire Freedman

illustrated by

Alison Edgson

Good Books

Intercourse, PA 17534
800/762-7171
www.GoodBooks.com

Hare loved bears.
He liked big bears, little bears,
hairy bears and scary bears.
   "If only I could find a bear,"
said Hare. "If only I could catch one!
The hairier and scarier the better!"

So Hare bought a book: *The Best Book of Bear Hunting*. He opened his book and took a look.

"Rumbly Rabbit!" called Hare. "I need you for a Very Important Bear Hunt!"

"A Bear Hunt?" said Rumbly Rabbit. "How do you hunt for bears?"

"It's all in my book," explained Hare. So he turned the page, and they took a look.

"Are you sure you want to find a bear, Hare?" said Rumbly Rabbit.

"Of course!" Hare said. "The hairier and scarier the better! Look, I've found a fishing net, a flashlight and a piece of string. What's next?"

They turned another page in Hare's book and took a look.

STEP 3

TRAILING YOUR BEAR

Now bears are not always easily found, so look out for pawprints on the ground.

Crouch down low but please beware—
THE BIGGER THE PAWPRINT,
THE BIGGER THE BEAR!

"I don't think I like the sound of Bear Hunting," said Rumbly Rabbit anxiously. "I hope we don't find any bear prints!"

"Over here!" called Hare excitedly. "I've found some!"

"Oh dear!" said Rumbly Rabbit. "They must belong to a VERY hairy, scary bear. Now what?"

They turned another page of Hare's
book and took a look.

STEP 4

WHAT TO LOOK OUT FOR

BEARS like to scratch on a favorite tree, it sharpens their claws quite nastily.

THEIR nails stay as sharp as the teeth in their jaws.

The deeper the scratch marks, the sharper the claws!

"I really don't like the idea
of Bear Hunting!" cried Rumbly Rabbit.
"Let's go back!"
   "Not now!" cried Hare excitedly. "We're
on the trail! And look what I've found!"
   Rumbly Rabbit looked. "Oh no!" he cried.
"Now what do we do?"
   "I'll tell you," said Hare. "It's all in my book."

So they turned another page
and took a look.

Rumble Grumble!

"Shh! Did you hear that?" whispered
Hare excitedly. "That sounds like a very
hungry bear to me!"

"Hear it?" trembled Rumbly Rabbit. "I was
almost deafened by it! Quick, Hare, let's
take another look in your book!"

STEP 6

MEETING YOUR BEAR

MEETING your bear can be quite shocking, don't let him see that your knees are knocking.

SUCK in your tummy and try to look thinner, and hope that he's already eaten his dinner!

"Yikes!" gulped Rumbly Rabbit. "Look over there, Hare!"

"Where?"

"It's a BEAR!"

"HELP! We'll never catch HIM with a fishing net
and a piece of string!" trembled Rumbly Rabbit.
"Just watch me try!" cried Hare.
"I'm HUNGRY!" growled the bear.
Then, suddenly...

"Dinner's ready," called Mommy Bear.

"It's bear-sized beans on bear-sized toast."

"Yummy!" said Little Bear. "Must go!"

"Come back!" called Hare.
Poor Rumbly Rabbit was too weak to speak!
"Oh no," cried Hare. "I can't lose
my bear—that's not fair!"

Quickly he took another look in his book.

STEP 7

WHAT BEARS LIKE TO EAT

A HUNGRY bear with an appetite will eat up any food in sight.

And all bears like baked beans on toast

But love bouncy hares and rabbits the most!

Rumbly Rabbit quickly grabbed Hare's paw.

"Run for it, Hare. There's no time to look. It's lucky those bears have not read your book! For if they did, I bet they'd try to make a hare and rabbit pie!"